Dedicated to my dear departed mother,
Margaret Nell "Margie" Mitchamore Chessher
She used to love my stories,
even the lies, sometimes.
And, throughout my career as a journalist,
always bragged about her son, the writer,
to anyone who might lend an ear,
voluntarily or not.
Love you, Mom!

Cutting It Short

A Collection of Short and Short-Short Stories

by Earl Chessher

2nd Edition, October 2012

ISBN: 978-1-300-35160-3

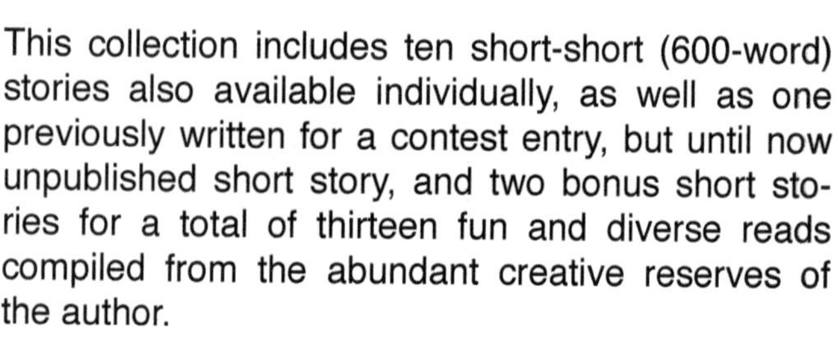

This collection includes ten short-short (600-word) stories also available individually, as well as one previously written for a contest entry, but until now unpublished short story, and two bonus short stories for a total of thirteen fun and diverse reads compiled from the abundant creative reserves of the author.

A Warm Rain

I heard thunder. Walking to the front door, opening to let in the fresh air and cool breeze, I started to warn the kids to come in. They were in the front yard, laughing and cutting up something fierce, dancing like little spirits in the fresh spring rain. Again I opened my mouth to call them inside but memories overtook me.

Suddenly I saw myself out there playing in the warm, gentle rain. I saw the kids I hung out with and my first real girlfriend. We were all cavorting, some ignoring calls from parents up and down the block. I remember one boy who wasn't at all satisfied with the amount of rain coming down so he had grabbed his dad's water hose from next door and stretched it all the way to our yard. We were already good and wet but the hose helped, I guess.

My kids had a good crowd with them as well, but there were no water hoses added to the mix. They were having plenty of fun, splashing in mud puddles forming where the grass hadn't taken well to the soil. Dancing turned to Red Rover as they took turns trying to break through lines of kids linked arm-in-arm. The cavorting progressed to another game that called for grabbing someone and spinning them until they fell onto the ground, hydroplaning through wet grass and mud. I chuckled as I watched them rise up out of the mud. all spattered, spitting out grass. Then they'd go at it again, and again.

I could picture Helen out there with me. Oh I had such a crush on that girl. She was the most beautiful thing my eleven-year-old eyes had ever seen. Skinny as a rail, with two big teeth up front and ears that flapped when she moved. But to me, well, what did I know back then? I thrilled each time we connected, even if the head bumps actually hurt. I remember hitting so hard one time that she started crying and got mad at me. I stood there in the rain, crushed.

The kids looked toward the door where I stood. They all of a sudden stopped yelling, screaming, cavorting. Just stood there in the rain, the mud rinsing away, looking at me all wide-eyed and smiling. Then my youngest called to me to come out and play in the rain with them. I can't believe I did. Walked out there in my cotton shirt and jeans, new sneakers and let them have their way with me. I wound up in the wet grass and mud myself, rolling over and over as they pushed me toward the ditch. I allowed them to dump me into the raging torrent there.

We stayed away from the ditches when I was a kid. Our parents had convinced us of all sorts of evil things that lurked in that muddy water; broken glass, icky bugs, germs. Didn't keep us from wading later after the rains stopped, but we didn't swim in it. That didn't matter to me at the time. What mattered was that Helen was angry. Twice I approached. Twice rejected. Then, the pain gone, she reached out and took my hand and smiled. I was back in heaven.

"You're such a nut!" my wife yelled. She'd been watching a grown man acting like an idiot in the front yard, playing in the rain with his kids. I got up, went to her and made her shriek with a muddy hug, driving the kids wild.

"I love you, Helen," I said.

The Love Letter

Not a day of my life has gone by that I don't think of you. I've no doubt whatsoever that the single biggest mistake of my life was not working harder to keep us together, not doing whatever it takes to make things right. I miss how you make love, how it felt to be one with you. I miss you and I'm so very sorry I let life come between us.

Not a day goes by or a dream in the night that I don't relive our love, the soft caresses and sweet words spoken in passion and truth. I only ever experienced this with you, even since you. No other has come close, and sadly even when our relationship came to an end I knew that would be the case. It's true. I knew, yet here we are so long apart, lives that go on while my soul, at least, remained behind. With you.

Her hand went to her chest and rested there. Though it had been more than thirty years since any contact with him she instantly recognized the hand writing, sensed a revelation would be contained inside the plain, white envelope. She found a seat at the secretarial she kept in the hallway, sat down and took a deep breath before sliding one long nail along the edge. As she pulled the three sheets of paper from the envelop she realized she'd been holding her breath.

I'm writing this because I miss you. I miss the passion we had, the excitement life held for us. I miss winning a dance contest not so much because we were talented dancers, but because we were so, well, connected that those who judged couldn't help but give us points for being one. We were one in a special, unique, real way. It was the only time for me that, like the old song about one being the loneliest number, one was not. Now, for sure, I can prove the song.

Yes, I'm lonely. And I've missed you for all these years, wondering, wishing, denying myself the reality of our lives; that we've moved on and are no longer in the past. I miss how you smell, how you feel, the sensational softness of your skin and the luster of your beautiful, long black hair. I miss the way you laughed, in humor, and in pleasure, always a musical note to it.

One small teardrop fell from her chin. She didn't even know it was there until it struck the page, causing the ink to suddenly spread, the word "beautiful" to nearly disappear. She paused from reading to listen for a moment to the quiet of her house. It had never once felt so lonely, so empty here, even with the kids grown and gone, the husband off to whatever it is retired men do during the day.

But, I'm not sorry. No. I'm not sorry that we met, that we made love and that we had each other for such a brief moment in time that has lasted me decades. I'm not sorry that in a lifetime without you I can still, even today, tonight in my dreams, actually feel and hear you. Touch you. Taste you. See you. Forgive me for this. No, don't forgive me, for then, if I knew you had, I'd die from the heartache of knowing. I have always loved you. I regret that I didn't keep you.

She pulled a single sheet of stationery from the drawer, began to write a reply. But the words wouldn't come. She just reread the letter.

Playing Bridge

A guy doesn't really know what he's capable of until the moment something happens calling for a split-second decision. There's a hesitancy when it comes to doing something unnatural, without consciously debating the alternatives. Something like driving off a bridge above flooded rivers.

The wrong decision is usually made, resulting in more people dying or injured than necessary, mega-million-dollar lawsuits. This was the situation when Rand took the nobel way out, opting to go through a bridge railing, taking his chances in the raging waters below.

One minute he's approaching a long, two-lane bridge, not a worry, humming along to some mindless tune. The next seconds he's semi-aware of a huge rig approaching him as he commits to crossing. Then seconds become a slow-motion movie as he realizes the forty-footer is passing someone, *passing a car on a bridge for God's sake*! Then split seconds as he sees the car is full of kids, a luggage racks on top, piled high with boxes and cases and stuff.

Slow-motion turns to hyper-speed. Rand's body, in a reflexive action, takes the path of least resistance. Muscles jerk his pickup toward the guardrails. Slow motion returns. Rand feels himself go weightless as his vehicle tears through the flimsy barricade and soars into the air.

During that brief flight he has time to wonder if the family in the car was remotely aware of being near death, if they'd noticed the big-assed diesel hauling down the wrong lane of a two-lane bridge, if they'd seen or heard his scream as he went over the side in an effort to avoid a head-on collision, probable death for all.

Then came the fall, weightlessness turning into free-fall as he plunged toward the river. Rand's last conscious thought was that it was a good thing, maybe, the river was full and not low or dry. *I'd surely die then*, he thought, before slamming into what felt like a concrete slab. His head hit the windshield a second before the bag popped, preventing him from slicing his neck open. Things went dark.

Rand knew he couldn't have been out long because the cab wasn't flooded. The windshield had held in spite of his instant impact and punching into the river's unforgiving surface. He felt the water swirling around. It was still light outside but Rand couldn't tell his position during a few precious seconds of discombobulation. Then he realized he was upside-down.

With remarkable presence of mind he untangled himself from the airbag, unhooked his seatbelt harness, grabbed the passenger-side door handle, braced himself and kicked out the driver-side window. The pressure from the flooding water pushed him against the passenger door, nearly breaking his wrist as he pulled on the door release handle. He was shoved out in an instant.

Something hard and unforgiving slammed into his ribs, taking the air he'd sucked in before his escape. He nearly drowned before breaking the surface, then diving deep to avoid the truck now rolling after him in the river's surge. In spite of the fall, the collision, the near-drowning he survived and made his way to the river bank a couple of miles down-river from the bridge.

He was still laying there exhausted, laughing uncontrollably when emergency units arrived. When the medical guys gave him a puzzled look, Rand stopped laughing long enough to explain.

"I just keep thinking about the old joke where some guys in the back of a pickup drowned because they couldn't get the tailgate down."

Breaking In

Chester thought nothing of it when the call came in at about 8 p.m.. The caller hung up. He didn't get the call at 8:30 or another at 8:45. Chester was out for a few hours; dinner with his girl, then a bar-hopping spree with buddies, even if Chester did get lucky.

He didn't. He and four buddies hit every joint, closing the last one down when the owner, another friend, ran them out well past closing time. Nearly 3:30 a.m. Chester arrived home to discover his place had been hit. Every drawer was pulled out, bedclothes and mattress upturned, sofa and chair cushions ripped open. His clothing had been pulled out and thrown onto the floor.

So, after the initial shock, Chester picked up the phone and called the police. Two officers showed up first, about a half-hour after his call, then a detective. It was nearly 5 a.m. Nobody appeared to have had much sleep. The cops were sharp, sarcastic. The detective, even more acerbic, came close to accusing Chester of setting the whole thing up.

They were most interested that Chester had an extensive gun collection, that it had been mostly hidden, with a few good pieces openly displayed in a glass case. The case was a disaster, shattered, glass strewn everywhere, tracked throughout. Chester was totally pissed at the law, at himself and the unknown perpetrators, who'd added insult to injury by not only taking his gun collection, and quite a few knives as well, but totally destroying his home and belongings.

"We'll check for prints but there aren't gonna be any," the detective said. The two cops smirked at this. When Chester asked why not the detective explained these guys were hit-and-run specialists and "most assuredly" wore disposable gloves.

"They weren't here more than five, and there were at least three, if not more," he said. They call the place ... insider information or no ... if you don't answer, they'll call again in a half-hour or so, maybe again, figuring that based on the hour and no answer the place is empty. They'll case it for a half-hour after arriving then, if nothing, kick in the door, turn the place inside-out.

Chester remembered the hang-up. He told the detective. They play the answering machine, hear another couple of hang-ups.

"Told ya," the detective said. He left after warning

Chester that prized collections like his guns meant he'd be hit again when they figured the insurance had paid off and he'd replaced his collection. "Beware of repeated late calls, hang-ups," he said.

Some months later Chester was relaxing at home when the phone rang about 8:30 p.m. He answered. The caller hung up. Chester remembered. When two more calls came in, leaving no messages, he knew. Chester grabbed his baseball bat, turned out the lights and slid behind the sofa. He waited.

Chester heard the door give to a savage kick, in spite of the new deadbolt he'd installed. He listened as they headed directly toward his old hide. He heard one mutter: "Sumbitch didn't replace the display case," snorting a laugh.

They were in the hallway when Chester came up behind them and started swinging his bat. It was payback time. When he'd finished working them over, Chester squatted at the end of the hallway, picked up the extension and called the direct number the detective had given him.

Keeping a cautious eye on the unconscious intruders, Chester waited patiently for someone to pick up.

“They came back,” he said, when the detective answered. He listened to the detective for a minute.

“No,” he said. “They’ll still be here when you guys arrive.”

Fat, Black & Ugly

Cops and detectives surrounded a wooded gravesite where a body had been discovered. Detective Charles Stodley thought he smelled almost as bad as the corpse in the shallow grave. He was on one knee, at the edge of the trench, staring at a seriously decomposed body. This one hadn't been a challenge for his helper, but Stodley was still proud of him. More than thirty-five bodies discovered by the guy. He never missed a stiff.

He chuckled softly as unabated cursing flowed behind him. Stodley knew what had caused the commotion. He realized it wasn't him that smelled, or the corpse for that matter, it was his partner. Rising to his feet, the detective turned around ready to issue a command, but he was a bit late. Somebody had dangled his hand down while holding the rest of his burger and Fat Black and Ugly had chomped it down, nearly taking the man's fingers with it.

"You gotta do something about this ugly son-of-a...." but Stodley cut him off with a curt warning. "Don't call him that. FBU knows what it means and he'll take your legs out from under you, you give him grief." Everybody turned to stare at the seven-hundred-pound black Russian boar, looking steadily at the cop with the offensive language, waiting for him to finish his sentence.

"Nice hog," the man said, hoping his voice was soothing and comforting, lacking the anger he'd felt a second earlier. FBU didn't look at all convinced. Finally he chuffed and snorted, then tossing his head in disdain, walked over to stand beside his friend.

Two things that members of law enforcement knew about Fat Black and Ugly and his "daddy" was you didn't call him an ugly son of anything and you didn't yell at him for stealing your food, especially if you left it dangling down, knowing that guy was around somewhere. Oh, and one other thing, you never, ever appeared to make a threatening move on his daddy, Detective Stodley. Many a ripped trouser and uniform leg, along with a few inches of prime skin would be the price to pay for aggression, real or perceived.

Stodley and FBU had been together since the Russian boar was born. Being raised on a pig farm had lasting effects on the detective and he did love his hogs. Though he worked in the city, Stodley made his way occasionally to the rural areas of the state. On one such visit he was awed by the huge and intimidating beast one of his farmer friends owned. It was a very wild Russian boar. And it was mean. But Stodley could talk him down. That impressed the farmer so much he gifted the detective with a piglet from the latest litter sired by his pride and joy.

Stodley made a pet out of FBU, and knowing how ultra-sensitive a hog's sense of smell could be, figured he could train the animal to sniff out dead bodies buried in suspected wooded or field dumping grounds by people who liked killing people. If hogs could be trained to sniff out truffles, Stodley figured he could get Fat Black and Ugly to do the same thing, only with decayed human bodies. Victims of murder.

FBU was basically a clean creature. Sure, if you left them in a small pen with no place to roam hogs would start stinking up the place. But FBU had the run of serious acreage on the Stodley property. And the detective kept his charge clean. He knew the department would give him grief otherwise.

With the discovery of his tenth lost body, FBU's position on the force was a given. At twnty-five, he'd become legendary. Now, with more than thirty-five finds to his credit, not one law enforcement officer in the department, heck in the county, in fact in the whole damn state, thought they could ever find a missing body anywhere without FBU.

Thus began the legend of Fat Black and Ugly the cadaver-sniffing Russian boar. His legend and popularity grew to the point that one day he became the character of a full-length novel, bringing Stodley along for the ride.

Bad Dreams

Bad dreams happen to good people. Play on words? You bet, but that doesn't make it a lie. Bad dreams do happen to good people and I'm going to share one with you. Get ready to never sleep again, never crawl into your bed without first looking under the it, under the covers and without plugging in a nightlight at every socket in the room.

My dad used to tell me that young men dream dreams and old men see visions, something that came from the Bible I think. I'm not sure the difference now, and I certainly wasn't sure back then, but this I know: bad dreams are totally scary. They make you wet the bed and scream without making a sound.

They cause you to fly over the tops of monsters but drag you down when you try to run, like sprinting through quicksand. They make you whimper in your sleep, causing you to wake up wondering why all the night lights are burned out. And they make you smell things. Yeah, bad dreams have bad smells. And during the worst of bad dreams you really can feel things touching you, pulling at you, messing with your hair and trying to crawl into your eyes, ears and nose.

Things that feel like worms, but are bigger. Much bigger. Gigantic and monstrous, huge and slimy, dark, dangerous demons. And you can't always fly over them or run from them. Sometimes you don't wake up in time. Sometimes they catch you and when they crush you in their grip or bite you with their huge teeth flashing from a mouth full of foul breath, it hurts.

Really!

Mom would always be baking and cooking stuff. She used stuff she called extracts that smelled like almonds or vanilla beans, lemon or peppermint, chocolate or coconut. They were pleasant smells, during daytime, when she was cooking and baking, mixing and opening and closing the oven door.

But they didn't smell good at night when everything was quiet and the night lights burned out. Not when you woke up with the intense taste of almond extract burning your throat, choking you, or when the smell of peppermint was so powerful it was impossible to breathe in so you could scream out loud.

Nighttime monsters aren't supposed to smell like mom's cooking. And mom's cooking isn't at all scary! Well, maybe her liver and spinach. Or when she and dad would enjoy a glass of buttermilk and cornbread. Yikes! That's what monsters in the middle of the night should smell like, cooked greens, cornbread and buttermilk. But not almond or peppermint extract. On the night I was attacked by three monsters, all smelling like almonds, peppermint and lemon I literally kicked holes in the sheets. I ran but got nowhere fast as the slimy tentacles wrapped themselves around my churning feet, binding my ankles. Tentacles, not the sheets that my parents insisted the next morning were wet from a burdened bladder and torn by an overactive dream.

I wasn't convinced. Not at all. What about the fact that those monsters crawled from under the bed and clawed, bit and grabbed me, tearing the sheets? Why did they smell bad like the good stuff mom cooked with, but not good like her cookies and cake or pie? Why couldn't I fly over them, or run from them, or scream for mom and dad in the middle of the night? Why did one of them come out of the dark closet. There, see, the door is still open!

No more sweets for you at bedtime, they said.

Don't Get Caught

The hardest thing in the world for a teen-ager to learn is to not get caught doing something wrong. Not as in a very bad thing, but doing something their parents have specifically nixed. *Rules for Teens*, if there were such a book, stipulates kids between the ages of thirteen and seventeen must learn how to sneak out, act up, drink at parties and drag race their dads' cars without getting caught.

Fat chance of that happening. Dad's car is a big, heavy clunker that only goes fast if you start from the top of a hill. Not many hills around here.

Some of that stuff has changed over the years but essentially the rules are the same. Be home by 8 p.m. school nights, 10 p.m. Friday nights. Leave a phone number where you'll be. Don't turn off your cell. No drinking! No smoking! No drugs! Well, it's just that there's a lot more to the drug scene now than seems there was in years past. Doesn't matter the crime, The Rule is "don't get caught!"

To hear my dad talk about it, getting caught was hard enough to avoid when you only had to contend with gossipy neighbors, creepy, nosey brothers and bratty sisters, or grownups who didn't know how to mind their own business. My parents had it made.

Now, do something wrong and it's all over Facebook, or somebody has to Twitter you out, or worse ... text your girlfriend and upload a picture of you accidentally hugging some girl, or a guy. Worst photo I ever got hit with was one somebody took of me puking up my guts.

I told my parents I was sick with the flu and they made me go to that party anyway. No! I hadn't been drinking! I was sick! I don't think they believed me. Besides, pictures can be faked, you know.

Parents are sneakier now than they were back in the day, from what Dad says. Mom keeps reminding him that they "did stuff" but never really comes out with what they did. I mean "stuff" is still the word I use when I don't really want to go into details about why my teacher kept me after school. Universal language? I don't think so. I think when Mom says "stuff" it's code for dad to not linger too long in glory days from the past.

"Don't glorify it, for God's sake!" I once heard Mom say to Dad late at night when they thought I was asleep.

Glorify what? I always wondered. They are so boring, always talking about some political thing that's happening now that never would have "back in the old days when protests really meant something. Back when politics got changed because of us!" Political or not, if I "protest" about anything they start telling me how ungrateful I am.

I'm still working on not getting caught. It's a serious challenge. Today's moms can hear you whispering in the dark confines of your bedroom, in the closet, with the lights out, a blanket over your head and the doors closed. Middle of the night.

"Tell her goodnight, turn off your cell and get to sleep," Mom yells from her downstairs bedroom. We weren't even talking. Just sitting there listening to each other breathe. Mom can hear me breathing?

Moms can also see for miles and they now have eyes in the backs of their heads. Dads read odometers and measure gas. They install spyware on your computer. Next they'll be reading my mind.

BRB, Mom just yelled at me to quit writing this stuff. Damn!

Jody Learns to Shoot

Jody was born and raised where hunting and fishing is a way of life. From the time he first learned to talk, every year Jody asked for a rifle.

"Dad, when can I have a gun?"

"When you're old enough," dad said.

"When's that?" emphasis on that.

"Tell me again how old you'll be?" Dad asked.

"Thirteen?" It wasn't a question, but Jody was hopeful, yet doubtful.

"Maybe then," dad said.

Jody wasn't particularly pleased. "Next birthday" was four months off. A long, long period in kid time. Nearly as long as waiting for Christmas or summer vacation. But he didn't push it.

Two months gone. Dad hadn't said a thing. Three months and still no word. Finally, it was a week away. Jody would bite his tongue when he heard dad talk about hunting trips with the guys — dad's friends that Jody's mom referred to as "immature jerks" whatever that meant. Jody suspected "immature" wasn't more complimentary than “jerk” He’d used jerk some himself, describing guys at school.

Jody heard his parents having a loud discussion. He asked if they were arguing.

“No, honey,” mom reassured with a hug. “We’re just having a discussion.” Jody went to bed bewildered. Still no word. Birthday Saturday brought the smell of baking cake. Jody saw his dad drinking coffee, newspaper flopped across his plate. Mom was beautiful, even with flour on the tip of her nose.

“Happy birthday!” they said. Dad roughed up his hair. Mom gave him a hug transferring some of that white stuff from her face to his. Dad pulled mom onto his lap. He must have goosed her or because she squealed and jumped up.

“You boys go!” she commended. “Stop stomping. If my cake falls ...” Jody knew that was a bad thing.

Wrapped packages were on the family room table, nothing long enough to be a rifle. Dad cranked the engine and they left. They soon arrived at a small woods where his dad went to hunt. Dad pulled his old .22 cal. rifle out. They walked for a bit, then his dad stopped, knelt down and handed his old rifle to Jody.

"Let's shoot some cans," dad said. "See what you can do."

Jody shot a bunch of cans. Dad told him it wasn't a bad score. On the way home dad told him this boring story about how when he was thirteen he'd begged Jody's grandfather for a rifle. He talked about learning to shoot, and gun safety: "A lot like I've done with you," dad said.

Dad pulled his truck over, killed the engine and looked at Jody.

"I'm proud of you, Jody. You've waited patiently and haven't bugged me about wanting a gun for months. You handled the rifle well and shot accurately, and used good safety."

He pushed the empty rifle over to his son.

"That rifle means a lot to me son. Not as much as you, but it's very special because my dad thought I was ready for one and he put a lot of faith and trust in me. It wasn't just having a rifle, it was the look on my dad's face when he gave it to me. I knew he was proud."

Dad gestured to the rifle now leaning against his son's leg.

"It's yours son. Not a new one but a very special one to me, for a very special son," dad said.

Jody beamed all the way home. No new rifle would ever mean as much to him as that old gun his dad loved, and the words he said as he gave it to him.

Body, It Be Rising

It's a wee bit cold in the humid bayou of Louisiana for crocodiles but don't let that worry ya none, dere's plenty of alligators 'round take meat off dem bones what find their way into dat water. Like dere's not other critters do the same, munchin' on pretty much any poor, sad thing wanders in too fer.

Turtles'll eat anythin' an' most fish, especially cat. Bottom feeders nasty as rats with gills dey are. Dere be all matter things roamin' dat water 'n grass, seekin' ta find somethin' ta eat. Findin' it too, I tell ya. Lotta people back in dere as well. Most of 'em would just 'bout eat anythin' what moves.

Dere's stuff on da bayou might nary seem fit fer humans, but right nourishin' if ya knows how ta fix it. E'er eat poke salad? I din't think so but Daddy Ransom says ain't much better than that stuff long's you pour off first water an' boil it again. Make ya sick otherwise, but done right tastes 'bout as good as a pot of turnip greens. Especially if you toss in a chunk of salt pork.

But ain't here ta tell 'bout food 'n stuff, or whut eats whut, how ta fix it. Gonna tell ya 'bout somthin' so strange ’bout dis bayou ’n da people livin’ dere ya won’t believe half of it. Can’t be bothered with that. I know it be true. Seen myself, or wouldn’t tole you nuthin’, just kept my big ol’ mouth shut.

Leonard wuz jest about da biggest, baddest man e’er hunt ‘gators. Din’t matter be the right or wrong side of da law. He hunt ‘em and cut ‘em. Make a buck off pretty much every part. Make sum of da finest boots you’d hope to own, hatbands, belts, even wallets. Dey mostly for visitors whut’s got money. Ain’t too many ’round where Leonard lived needed no wallet. Ne’er had no money ta put inside. Whut’s da use, right?

Dat man turned up missin’. Gone ‘bout ten day. Folk knew he be out dere on or under dat bayou, probably dead or ‘gator food. Tucked under a sunken snag where dem monsters stash their food. Like rich folk be likin’ their beef aged, rotted ya ast me, ‘gators prefer it rich and flavorful.

Wuz no doubt Leonard good and gone, rotten down dere in dat bayou. Done met ’is maker or da devil, ast me. He ’ad bayou family, he did. Wuz no surprise dey decided Leonard needed findin’. Bunch of ‘em set out after dark to whereabout dey knowed he hunted ’is ‘gator.

Din't matter nobody tole 'em dere no use lookin' cause Leonard, well he be 'gator steak. No never mind dat he wuz long gone, dey gonna bring him back. Give dat man a decent and proper burial. Had my own doubts 'bout dat.

Dere we all wuz, sittin' an' standin' in our pirogues, hummin' an' chantin', makin' all sort scary noises. Women held lanterns high. Men beat on stuff din't sound nuthin' like no drum. If Leonard ain't dead and climbs up outta dat water, he gonna be when he hears all dat racket.

He wuz dead, but ain't nuthin' took no bite outta 'im. Leonard looked jes' like he 'us sleepin'. E'erbody said he musta falled in an' drowned. Buried him right an' proper. I'm a gotta tell ya, no way dat man be gone dat long whut sumptin' didn't eat 'im. I shore nuff ain't gonna be doin' no whistlin', hummin' or bangin' on things out on that bayou alone at night.

No sir.

Spiderwebs

Jeremy didn't care for spiders. He hated their webs. Where there's a web there's a spider. Run into one at night, there's no telling where that spider had gone, likely in your hair. The bad thing is once you run into a spiderweb, if it didn't get in your hair, or go down the neck of your shirt or climb into your armpit! Well your whole body felt like it was crawling with them.

Not only that, but you just knew it was a female and had just distributed babies all over you. Why would your skin be crawling all over the place? Why'd you feel them in your ears, up your nose, scampering across your eyeballs? Jeremy remembered only ever seeing just one spider per web, but that didn't mean there weren't legions of them hiding on the outer edges.

Spiders, Jeremy hated. String, he loved. Any kind of string. Kite string. String to roll newspapers with. String off feed sacks and bags. You have to carefully unravel those or the string keeps breaking. Had to be real string, not nylon or plastic twine. Real, genuine string you could cut or break with your hand if you pulled hard enough.

String was just loads of fun and Jeremy learned to do so many things with it. He could wrap it around dad's old spinning tops, give them a toss and a spin. They'd go around and around for a long time. Maybe hours. Well, not hours but long enough it seemed like hours.

He also used it to refit his dad's old Yo-yos. String came in handy if you wanted to tie something up in a bundle. Jeremy used his dad's old golf balls, gluing and wrapping string around them until they were the size of a baseball or softball. Jeremy and his buddies could play for hours before those balls fell apart.

Yes, string is very useful, interesting and fun. Jeremy learned he could do many different things with string, including get into trouble with it.

Once, after returning home from a visit to his grandma's Jody took the prize. Knowing of his love for string, Grandma would save every piece of string she came across, knotting it end-to-end and wrapping it until sometimes, depending on how long between trips, she sometimes had a ball of string nearly the size of a basketball waiting for him. Jeremy was beside himself. Whatever could he do with all that string?

What could he tie up, create or bundle with what

looked like enough string he could have made a mummy of himself with it? Hey! He thought. A mummy! Nope, Halloween was gone and they'd just returned from Thanksgiving dinner at Grandma's.

Then Jeremy remembered how much he hated spiderwebs. But he figured it would be pretty cool to see how big of a spiderweb he could create in the house. So, while his mom and dad were next door playing dominoes, Jeremy started using his imagination. He knew spiders started with long strands stretching from things, then they'd go around from strand-to-strand making the center parts. By the time he was done the entire front room was a mass of string spiderweb.

That was when, exhausted, Jeremy fell asleep on the floor, beneath his giant spider web. Mom and dad returned home to a quiet house, whispering while one of them reached for the light switch. Must have been his mom because by the time she threw the switch dad had walked right into the giant web, pulling down lamps, picture frames and chairs.

"Jeremy!" his dad roared.

Busted!

I never got into any serious trouble in high school. Yeah, right. Never got caught anyway. Never, that is, until I talked my sweet mother, who knew how good I'd been all those years in school, into letting me skip school on Senior Day and go surfing.

Sure, they're not all that to the big bongos who catch the waves off California, Hawaii, or maybe Australia, but I was content with the ripples off Galveston Island, Texas. My favorite story, however, was taking the big ones raised by the late great Hurricane Carla. Yeah, I guess that was years ago, huh?

Years ago, when myself and a couple of buddies shared roof tops with snakes, both species trying to stay afloat along with a lot of Galveston's structures that year. Carla was nasty, but we weathered it, rode out the storm and the eye, and the blast that came later. We were too stupid, I guess, to consider the danger, and too young to die.

But I rarely got caught, or into serious trouble, until Senior Day. Well, OK, there was the plastic model car thefts I got nabbed for at the local shopping center. And, come to think of it, the time I played chicken across a busy intersection, but forgot that there was only a deep ditch on the other side, not to mention the heavy flow of traffic. Didn't hit, or get hit by, any vehicles on that one, but I did manage to go headfirst into the ditch. Who should come to my assistance but an off-duty highway patrol officer who took mercy upon me and let me go. He saw the redemption of blatant fear on my face.

I still had to face the folks because somebody was going to have to help me get the car — did I tell you it was the family wagon — out of that ditch. Oh, I paid for that one, I did. Paid in more ways than one.

You gotta understand something about me and my family. I experimented with things some. OK, I experimented with things a lot, but I was smarter than the average student and almost always managed to convince most adults, even if they didn't come across as adults, mature ones anyway, that I was an honest, responsible, level-headed guy. So I tended to get my way about things more often than not.

That included talking my mom into letting me skip school on Senior Day. And, it all would have worked out pretty good had I not decided it would be more fun if I took a few of my buddies — the Hurricane Carla Club

— with me to Galveston. We'd make the trip down Highway 45 and be on the beach in no time, I thought.

In hindsight I would have had all the fun and company I wanted if I'd made the trip alone, maybe even have gotten lucky and scored some. You know what I mean, don't you? Found a friend, stayed warm, tripped the light fandango, temporarily fallen in love. Experimental sex folks. Gads, doesn't anybody remember the good old days? The days of raging hormones and blatant urges toward copulation?

That wasn't to be, however. It wasn't to be because I decided that I could become invisible, drive up to the high school parking lot, get the word out and head off with a car full of friends and adventurous new acquaintances ready for a balls-to-the-wind assault on the island beaches.

Because I was so blatant about it, not bothering to share whispers and establish secret meeting places, I guess I thought nobody but my buddies would take notice. There were a few problems with this approach. First, most of my buddies were going to have to sneak home, sneak in and back out with their boards, swimming suits, food and stuff. And, of course, we had to line up a few girls to keep us company. And, none of these people had the permission I'd been granted by mom to skip school in the first place. We're talking double, triple, jeopardy here.

Well, let me tell you, everybody noticed but us.

Mom was pretty cool about it when I returned with a car full of kids. We needed to figure out how to get all the boards attached to that old Plymouth with the push-button transmission so they wouldn't fall off on the way to the beach. We needed to stock up on food and towels — some of the kids hadn't been able to sneak in or out of their homes.

We were about to depart when I heard a hard, firm officious knock on the front door. I suspected. I exchanged a few glances with some of my friends. The girls were all wide-eyed. All of stood there in various frozen positions, afraid to breathe, afraid to move.

Mom answered the door. The high school principal, a truant officer and a, gasp, regular police officer were standing outside, demanding that mom open the door and let them in. Mom, being part afraid of authority, part respectful of authority figures, and totally innocent of the law, finally moved to let them. This, after receiving the harsh warning that if she had been involved in this childish behavior, she too would find herself in trouble with the authorities.

Hey, nobody threatens my mom. I came forward, jerked the door open wider and told the small crowd of officials my mother had nothing to do with it, that I'd intimidated her and faked being sick, so she kept me out of school.

My group, meanwhile, had made its escape. Some went out windows. Others hid in closets. A few made their way to the bomb shelter — remember those — in our back yard. A few went over the backyard fence and made their way out of the neighborhood. Me, I bravely confronted these tough guys who were bracing my innocent mother.

I denied any knowledge of names or identities of others who were allegedly involved in my school skipping. Some of the kids, however, were noticed as they climbed out windows or slammed back doors while making good their temporary escapes. Most were eventually found out, snitched on or turned themselves in.

Some were put on detention as a few weeks of school remained. Others were expelled for a couple of days. A few received mild slaps on the wrists after giving up names of others. A couple were never caught, rendering them the heroes of future stories about the Great Senior Day Escape.

Being the uncooperative instigator, I was kicked out for a week. My grades were such, and most of my teachers sympathetic enough to allow me to do some undercover makeup work, that losing a week of school this close to the end of the school year — my senior year at that — didn't cause me much grief.

But yes, I'd been busted. Busted big time. So, hanging my head in shame, I walked out to the car, threw a cooler full of sodas, wieners and sandwich spread in the back seat, a bag of chips on the floorboard, got in and drove to Galveston. There, I surfed a bit, flirted a lot, got sick eating too many dogs with too much mustard, and fell in love with a cute gal who wasn't bashful at all about being a true redhead. Or proving it.

Gosh, I wonder if that's on my record somewhere, along with the time I got busted for allegedly stealing quarters from newspaper racks around the town? Allegedly, being the key word here.

Eyes on the Door

The moment became a series of moments. The series of moments a habit. The habit a ritual. Abe felt funny one night, waking up after a couple hours of sleep and a stupid bad dream and sensed that something was on the other side of his front door. The practice started with a strange goofy dream about something with a huge pair of eyes, something that didn't climb over, crawl under or squeeze through the wrought-iron security fence surrounding the retirement community Abe lived in. In his dream, *something* simply walked through the fence as if it wasn't there.

Then whatever it was just stood, inches from the screen door guarding the multi-pane wooden front door with its collection of key lock, deadlock and inside hasp secured with a very expensive brass padlock. Not that Abe was a chicken, or a wus, he just appreciated good protection. With the rampant anarchy all about. Drug dealers, human traffickers, child stealers and bleeding heart liberals killing baby killers during this election year, it was simply a good idea to have multiple levels of security at windows and doors.

He was particularly pleased that his place had only

one entrance. The front door. One regular entrance and three windows. That left him with few places to have to establish credible security. The bad thing about this arrangement, Abe realized, was that it left him with no alternate escape route either. So, while he might be adequately protected from home-jackers he was also pretty much in a corner if it came to having to bolt from a non-existent back door.

No panic room either, unless you wanted to qualify the bathroom. There were times when Abe sat in there and literally panicked because he couldn't force a good BM no matter how hard he pushed. Abe also panicked in there on those rare occasions when he didn't have to push at all but rather had to hold back to prevent blowing out the toilet bowl. The panic came when the full deposit washed out over the floor as the commode overflowed.

There was the closet, half the size of his bedroom, but it didn't have a door. And being a somewhat dedicated hoarder Abe had too much stuff in there to allow for a good "hideyhole" anyway. Whatever or whomever came in through the front door would take all of about one minute to find him, bathroom or closet, and then he'd have to fight. Abe didn't mind fighting. A good confrontation was something to be relished, but he knew he wasn't as able, fit or strong as he used to be and Abe feared that an intruder, unless it was some snot nosed, dope headed kid, would make short work of him if Abe didn't get in the first three blows. Or four.

He'd won more fights than lost over the years, but touching on seventy wasn't the age to try and reclaim a championship belt or anything. Thugs today cheated with bats, boards, knives and guns — not that Abe hadn't cheated a time or two in a fight — but there were no rules of engagement, no gentlemen's approach to fisticuffs in this day and age. And Abe hated pain.

And pain is what happens when you get cornered in your own home by anarchy-flamed human rats or some other scuzzy human feces bent on doing you no good, taking your worthless stuff and making you sorry for having ever been born. So anyway, notwithstanding his desire for security, Abe developed the habit-ritual of going to his front door, carefully parting the mini-blinds and peeking through one of the glass panes onto his lighted front porch, past the sidewalk and its light, through the wrought-iron security fence and into the park beyond.

He could no longer see well enough past that to

worry about the street on the other side of the park or the dark, most of them anyway, houses squatting near the distant curb. As far as Abe was concerned it was bad enough having to worry about his own well-being without having to think about what might or might not be happening across the street — too far to run to and too far for him to yell a warning loud enough to scare or warn anybody deep into their snores over there.

The first time he groaned his way out of the sofa bed he used in his living room — Abe thought it best that he be as close to the front door as possible in the event something or somebody did ever come through it late at night while he was sleeping. About all the cedar heartwood walking stick, a cudgel really, was good for was to give him bruises and a sore back whenever he rolled over on it. Be that as it may, Abe felt much better sleeping with his weapon of choice than he did on the nights he forgot to tuck it in with him.

The sawed-off Mossberg loaded with double-ought posed a serious concern because Abe often flexed his fingers in his sleep — a lot — and could just imagine the consequences of that, blowing off his toe, foot or something of major importance to him, still, in the still of the night. That wouldn't do at all. Neither would sleeping with his old Army issued Colt under the pillow. Shooting himself in the middle of a major nightmare simply was not an option, thus the walking stick.

Don't think Abe hadn't thought about the probability of whoever came in the door in the middle of the night intending to do him harm and injury using his own weapon against him. Abe knew he'd likely sleep right through any home invasion, earthquake or an engine falling off some plane and landing right in his freaking lap. But, in light of the uneasy feelings and the ever-increasing ritual of nighttime observations through the interstices of his mini-blinds. You know.

Anyway, the first time he rolled out of that torture chamber mattress and took a peak there was nothing to see. The park was covered in fog. Some weird lights barely pierced the thickness of it. Nothing stood on his porch staring back at him and all was well with the world — as much of it as he could see anyway.

So it was back to bed. And Abe distinctly remembered his dreams during the remainder of the night improving — a lot. He dreamed about this gal or that one, most of the ones he let get away, slip through his grasp, but mostly he bypassed the ones he'd married or his mother-in-laws. He remembered one of these women particularly well, the one with the huge, glimmering golden green eyes. But then it was all ruined because just about dawn, as he was coming up out of his fitful rest, those eyes grew large as saucers and once again that thing walked right through the security fence and was standing at his front door, staring. Waiting for him to pull down a blind and ...

... and what, Abe didn't know because, of course, he woke up with a jerk, grabbed his walking stick. rolled off the mattress of torture and jerked open the blinds only to see ...

... nothing!

***

Moxie didn't know where her name came from. Nobody from her own kind nor The Others, ever bothered calling her anything, much less Moxie. It was just what she was supposed to be called, she supposed.

She only knew that she was always compelled to come to that front door and stand there, staring, waiting. But nothing ever happened. She'd been doing it for nearly a year and still nothing. But Moxie never questioned the need for doing this, nor refrained from doing as whatever compelled her, compelled her.

So, on certain nights that had no rhyme or reason, no weather-related basis, no significant change in the moon, the stars or the time, Moxie stood there at that front door and waited for some indication of why she was supposed to be doing this. That first time, her first night out of the woods, away from the deep dark recesses of the mountain cave, she stood and waited, then left, just as Abe pulled down a space between the mini-blinds and peered out.

By the time Abe had crawled back into his bed, Moxie had covered many a mile, returning to her cave and home, deep in the mountain woods, away from The Others but not with any of her kind either. Moxie was the only one of her kind. How she knew this she didn't know, only that it was indeed true. Sometimes, in the early morning hours, Moxie caught brief glimpses of a time before. Some moment of her existence when others like her played around on the mountains, in fear of nothing or The Others. Without purpose, it seemed, feeding off this animal or that one, drinking from melted snow, pools or streams high up in the San Bernardino Mountains.

But when Moxie tried to pull that into focus, the teasing images dispersed, went away and refused to give clarity to any past memory. So, mostly, Moxie just let it go and went on about her business, whatever that was. Mostly she slept inside her hidden redoubt, dreamed of cantankerous little old men living among The Others, then stood and stared at that front door when compelled to do so.

Just to be sure you know the difference, Moxie is nearly seven feet tall, covered with some kind of soft, reflective hair the color of pearl, like they used to paint some of those old Thunderbird cars. She has fairly delicate features, not all that feminine but certainly endowed with breasts and cute little cat-like ears that perch on each side of her upper temples. All she needs is a polka dotted bow to complete the look.

But, when she smiles it might be difficult to dwell on the cuteness because a smile makes Moxie look like those puppets on TV whose heads tilt back as they talk, looking for all the world as if they're going to split in half. And, Moxie's smile also reveals row-upon-row of tiny, needle-sharp teeth. Some of them, the longer ones along the sides, squirt out a kind of clear, viscous liquid when she tries too hard to make nice. For all her efforts at giving forth a pleasant greeting, anything and everything that gets to see this flees, often emitting high-pitched sounds that would unnerve the most unshakable of creatures.

Fortunately for most creatures Moxie prefers fish. And, fortunately for most creatures Moxie loves the water, so she pays no never mind to wading into a dark pool or stream and working for her dinner. Or breakfast, lunch or snack.

Whatever the composition of her hair and body, Moxie also doesn't have to veer or avoid obstacles. She can simply walk a straight line, getting from point A to point B pretty much faster than any other living creature. Trees, no problemo. Big, huge boulders, parked cars or boat trailers, da nada. About the only things Moxie cannot walk through without harm or danger, either to herself or whatever, are The Others and other creatures such as bear, deer, dogs or horses. Or cows. Moxie knows of this because she has made a mistake or two where she forget and mindlessly tried to go through a standing, sleeping bovine, causing serious consequences.

All she got was an upset stomach or it made her breasts hurt, but the cow always died.

So, whatever that is all about, Moxie tries to avoid, or remember to avoid attempting to walk through such creatures. Fish don't cause her stress, neither do crayfish, shellfish at the beaches or insects. Good thing to know, even if the other creature does not.

***

Abe made a day of it, several days in fact, getting a haircut at the local fluff shop where they never get it right and charge way too much. How hard is it, anyway, to zip that trimmer over the temples and scalp a few times? Zip, zip, whisk with a camel hair brush, getting trimmings all over your neck and shirt so that you itch for the next twelve hours, expect a ten buck tip in addition to the twenty-dollar haircut. Damn! Everything costs too much.

Abe hates having to buy the store brand carbonated drinks because the brands are all priced out of sight, and really don't taste that much better either. On the other hand, when he takes a chance on the store brand butter, cheese, beans or soap, there's definitely a difference. The cheese tastes like soap and the soap tastes like store brand bean soup.

But the checkout lady is cute. Young. Spry. Flirtatious. The only one, sadly, and usually there's a line of retirement age guys in Hawaiian shirts and young butt heads in muscle shirts with tats up to here, all standing in line, waiting for a chance to be noticed by The Sexy One. There is nobody in the other lines where anxious and flirtatious older women with sags, bags and dark circles under their eyes are perfectly willing to give a little extra attention in exchange for some in return. Only thing is, with any of them, sag and bag or cute and flirtatious, he gets tired of having to push his one-bag shopping spree to the side and double check the receipt because somewhere in there he was double charged or over charged.

Driving doesn't help things any, with all the road rage going on. Damned young ones acting like their parents' Honda has qualified for the Indy. Shooting birdies right and left, or cutting him off just before his turn. Abe was still pissed about having to go to the local clinic just a few days ago for an examination he couldn't afford, pay a extortion fee for an exam he didn't need so the gal in a white smock would up his blood pressure meds, keep him from having The Big One brought on by his own road rage.

Jesssh, Abe thought, just let me get home in one piece.

He arrived safe enough, but had to watch out for the

dog poop some of the residents leave lying on the side-walk — the sidewalk, mind you, not the grass where people don't usually walk. Maybe they don't have enough plastic bags to do the job, or are too damned inconsiderate and don't give a crap what their noxious little yappers drop behind. He missed two big ones though.

It was a great sense of relief to get inside with his meager groceries, put the fudge sickles in the freezer, the watered-down orange juice in the fridge door, the over-priced eggs in their little holders. He pulled open the silverware drawer and took out a tablespoon, the big one not one of those teaspoons manufacturers call table-spoons, grabbed the plastic jar of peanut butter — not filled to the top, mind you — and plopped down onto his recliner. Abe snapped up the remote and pointed it at the television. It made some kind of noise, then the tube — tube, screen, whatever — went from black to fuzzy to light and the right station, for once, played. The volume, for once, remained where he'd last set it.

But right after Abe dug into the peanut butter, pulling out a giant lump in his tablespoon, the game was preempted by another one of those stupid presidential debates. Dumb ass questions by fat, inarticulate broad-cast channel has beens, followed by stupid comments by the pompous prez, followed by articulate but strangely ineffectual replies by the candidate running against him. Abe pushed the off button, but what he really wanted to do was throw the remote at the screen. Only thing was he'd likely have to pay out the you-know-what for a universal replacement that wouldn't be programmed right after eight hours of trying, or the screen would crack. That would not work at all.

So, Abe grabs a magazine, one of those weekly news magazines that print slanted fiction reports on the local, national and world scene, slandering perfectly good government representatives on the conservative side while licking up the backsides of those bleeding heart liberals who want to give all his tax money to third world countries and places where they behead people, have all the oil and think of the good Ol' US of A as the great satan.

"Satan indeed," Abe muttered. He settled for revisiting a few good memories and licking the blob of peanut butter from his spoon.

Bored out of his skull, Abe decided to take a turn around the park outside his front porch. He nearly snapped off the gate key — probably because some jerk resident grandma let her grandkids swing on it or twist their key wrong, messing up the lock. But it worked, finally, and Abe found himself dodging more doggy poop on the public park sidewalks.

"Must be a shortage of plastic bags," he muttered. The next obstacle in his path and to his sense of quiet and solitude was a whole crowd of dog lovers hovering over the sidewalk, sitting on the only park bench available and continuously untangling leashes. Bad enough he had to go out onto the grass because they damn sure weren't going to pull on the leashes and get their dogs out of his way. Stepped right into a fresh pile. Abe made a point to wipe his shoe off on the walk.

Then, once again, it was his bedtime. The commode didn't overflow and the bathroom faucet turned off without a drip in sight. No toothbrush bristles came off in his mouth and the toothpaste tube didn't build up air pressure, spitting a glob of the stuff onto the medicine cabinet mirror. Makings for a good enough night, Abe thought.

Then came the dream.

***

Moxie felt compelled. So, making really good time that night, she found herself once again crossing the park, this time right in the middle of the sprinklers coming on. But no matter, being wet caused her no grief. She calmly and carefully crossed through the middle of four tree trunks, the fence and stopped just shy of Abe's screen door, and waited.

Oddly enough, not once in all her trips, not one single time in all the nights she'd covered the vast distance between the mountains and Abe's place, did Moxie attract attention. Not ever had one of The Others noticed her, or even looked her way, even when she did her walking-through-solid-objects thing. True, she was more attentive of her surroundings than it might appear if anyone did happen to notice, but still you'd think these creatures, or at least their dogs, might have bumped up against her at least once in all her trips. Not.

Here Moxie was, standing still, and wondering why, in front of Abe's front door. Waiting and watching, expecting that any day now the old guy would peek through his blinds and see her standing there, eyes the size of saucers and glowing golden green. Moxie wasn't sure exactly what she was supposed to do when that ever happened, but she thought that smiling might be the first action to take.

***

It was two o'clock in the morning when Abe, after two solid hours of tossing and turning, sat up in his sofa bed. He felt for his walking stick and found it partially wedged in his butt crack — no wonder it hurt him so much, disturbed his sleep — pulled it out from under himself, then turned around and let his legs bend at the knees, dangling his feet over the side, toes barely brushing the floor.

Abe propped his walking stick against the mattress, reached up and rubbed the sleep — sleep, ha! — from his eyes, then cautiously looked up at the front door. Wasn't hard to do, the damn thing was close enough he could reach it with his hand if he stretched a bit. But Abe wasn't inclined to stretch a bit. He felt a stronger sense of something standing there, on the other side, waiting than ever he had before. Grabbing his walking stick, Abe slapped it painfully against his knee. He wanted to make sure he was, indeed, awake and not still in the middle of one of his crazy nightmares. He was awake and his knee hurt to gosh all for a fact. Abe changed his mind about standing up on that side of the bed and having to walk around the end of the sofa bed, to the other side, then into the kitchen for a drink of water.

Instead, he rolled onto his back, swung his legs

around like a 19-year-old gymnast and sprung up into a sitting position on the opposite side of the bed, away from that front door. He pushed himself up, then shuffled toward the kitchen, started to open up the fridge door, then opted to not do that because the one time he didn't want it to work the damn inside light would sure as hell turn on, alerting whatever might be lurking on the other side of the blinds.

So, Abe opened the cupboard door, it didn't squeak at all, and retrieved a glass without clanking it against another, pulled it down from the shelf and reached to turn on the faucet. But he stopped mid-reach. The water running would probably be loud enough to alert whatever was probably lurking on the other side of the blinds.

Damn! Couldn't piss, too much noise. If he sat down to do it quietly, couldn't flush, too much noise. Couldn't turn on any other lights because that might alert something ...

... something he absolutely knew was standing outside his front door. Finally, after all this time of fearing, fretting, peeking and breathing in a deep breath followed by a massive sigh of relief, anything he did might alert whatever it was to his awareness. Goodness only knows what would happen then. So, if he was going to make noise that alerted anything, it was going to be pulling his Mossberg and Colt from the big closet stuffed with "hordable" shit, loading the damn things and then proceeding to his front door.

Abe winced at the click the double-barrel made when he cracked it open as quietly as possible. He slid in two rounds of double-ought, checked his Colt to make sure it was loaded. Not that it shouldn't be, he hadn't unloaded it the last time he shoved it full of bullets — Alzheimer's hadn't kicked in yet, by golly — but he couldn't for the life of himself remember if it was last week or the week before that he broke it down, cleaned it thoroughly then reloaded.

Satisfied, Abe carried the shotgun in the crook of one arm and his right hand dangled at his side, clutching the Colt, safety off. He became aware of the sweat rolling down, tickling his ears, flowing cold down the middle of his back, soaking into the waistband of his sleepers. He stopped at the entryway to his living room, where he slept so he could be closer to the front door in the event of an intruder, carefully propped the Mossberg against the doorjamb, grabbed the bottom of his t-shirt and wiped his face and forehead. He curled a piece of cotton around his forefinger and ran it around the back and under each ear, drying off the river of sweat running from his temples.

Looking up at the front door, then carefully back down at the shotgun, Abe reached for it and silently picked it up. Ah, he thought, not a sound. When he looked back up at the front door Abe could almost swear something on the other side of those blinds was trying to shine through.

Probably some jerk with one of those mega flash-lights doing something to freak him out, Abe thought. He also thought that if he walked over to the door, jerked it open and shoved the Mossberg in the joker's face he might be the one causing somebody to freak out. Maybe the butt head would pass out or drop dead from a heart attack. Would serve him right.

So, fortified for the rush, Abe walked rapidly up to the front door with its multi-locks then, remembered it was multi-locked and would not easily yield to being jerked open, or for that matter, kicked in from the other side. Instead, Abe reached up with the Colt and nudged open a space between the mini blinds and peeked out onto his lighted porch.

Nothing.

Maybe not, Abe thought with a major sigh of relief, but he was still going to sleep with both guns and the walking stick for what was left of the night. He placed guns and stick on the mattress then went to the fridge, pulled open the door, grabbed the orange juice carton and slugged down nearly a third of it.

Spying the cheese that tastes like soap, some wheat stone crackers that usually tasted as though they contained mostly stone, Abe grabbed them and carried his snack and orange juice to the sofa bed. There, after placing his goodies on the side table, used as a nightstand, he turned and peeked out through a space between two blinds one more time.

Nothing.

***

Moxie felt compelled to leave just as abruptly as she had been compelled to come. She'd been at Abe's front door for what seemed like hours, but it was just about two hours, from just past midnight until just past when she sensed something stirring on the other side. Sadly, she turned away and left. Moxie had thought for sure tonight was when she and Abe would get acquainted. She had even practiced her smile several times, thinking she finally had achieved just the right expression, one that would have possibly caused Abe to open his door and invite her in.

Just as Moxie passed through the iron security fence she turned and looked at Abe's door one more time. Her emotions got the best of her, kicking up the brightness of her golden green eyes to full intensity — close to the wattage of the cheap shop lights everybody buys at the discount stores and uses for lighting during a video shoot.

Not that Moxie would know that, particularly, but there were a lot of things that happened inside her head, thoughts from nowhere related to The Others and their strange behavior. Seemed there were many, many elements of thought, vision, even voices, that sometimes swarmed over her and though Moxie didn't come close to putting it together cohesively, she did carry an underlying sense of understanding about it all.

Watching her reflected eyes from the glass behind the screen door, Moxie realized she probably shined right through the screen door, wooden door with its many glass partitions and the slivers of metal, some kind of binds, hanging on the other side. Abe, yes, she knew his name somehow, probably noticed that, she thought.

Then Moxie turned away and walked across the park. She did not feel compelled to make the trek all the way back to San Bernardino, opting instead to walk through the walls of a nearby storage facility that had been locked up like, forever.

Moxie lay, relaxing, eyes without lids waxing and waning in intensity as she breathed in, then out. She saw nothing, except in her thoughts, it was simply the way her system worked, charging up the intensity from those saucer-sized orbs with each intake, dimming with each expelled breath. She yawned, mouth huge, needle teeth standing out starkly white against the darkness of her throat, the cavity behind lips and teeth. Far different from a smile, the yawn would have stopped the heart of any person who happened to witness it. Frightening, to say the least.

***

It was four o'clock in the morning when Abe gave it up. He absolutely could not sleep a wink after the earlier experience, and sleeping with all the guns and walking stick in his bed left very little hope for comfort. Every muscle and every joint banged like a banshee, ripping through his nervous system and brain like fillet knives wielded with abandon.

Another long, loud groan accompanied him into an upright position, knees bent, feet dangling, toes brushing the carpet. Abe glanced at the front door. He felt nothing, saw nothing. This time, with the porch light turned off, there was no comforting glow, nor disconcerting brightness of threatening flashlights from strangers outside. No sense of presence caused his already pounding heart to beat any faster. Or to stop beating altogether. That was a good thing.

But not for long because just as Abe stood and turned, his back to the front door, maybe three feet from the mini blinds protecting him from the outside world with the inadequacy of the current government, hell, pretty much every government administration since, well Eisenhower or Reagan, Abe felt it. He felt the hairs on the back of his neck rise. The skin on his face, arms, back and legs turned to ostrich hide, pimply bumps running wall-to-wall.

And he froze. No gun within reach. The walking stick lying there, stiff and brittle, just like one, any one, pick one, of his ex-wives. Out of reach. The pistol nestled safely under his ravaged pillow. His back to that damn front door. Well, at least all the locks were engaged. Right?

Abe began sweating again. His heart raced even faster, only barely slowing when he became pretty sure he had, in fact, locked and secured before laying back down earlier in the morning. But he had forgotten to leave on any lights and there was absolutely no glow leaking in from the window or door blinds. It looked like not only had he turned off his porch light, but the sidewalk lamp sitting on top of its seven-foot post must have blown as well. It was dark. Black.

And the last thing Abe wanted to do was turn and face his fears. The next-to-the-last thing he wanted to do was turn, part a space between two of those little strips of metal, put his eye to the crack and look outside. The last thing he wanted to do was see what it was that had been standing there all these nights, all these months, since the beginning of his ritual/habit. Addiction?

The night remained dark and when Abe turned to the front door he perceived no glow. There seemed to be no person outside with flashlights, shining them through his door, into his eyes should he decide to part the blinds and peer.

***

It was the right time, Moxie knew. So, without hesitation she pushed up from the floor of the storage unit, walked through the walls into the park beyond, and headed, compelled, to Abe's front door. She paused at the fence before passing through, kicked up the wattage in her saucer eyes, pulsing golden green against the frame of Abe's front door. She sensed that he was awake, standing even, but had not yet turned back to face his door again. He, Moxie felt, was fighting with his myriad fears in an attempt to ignore the door, not face his fright.

Moxie smiled at the thought. Good thing Abe hadn't picked that particular moment to peek through the blinds.

Then she walked through the fence, through Abe's front porch gate, stopped and stood at the bottom of the steps leading up to the smaller rise at the entrance to Abe's residence. As Moxie let out her breath the lights in her eyes dimmed nearly to darkness. She took in a great, deep, fulfilling breath, once again kicking up the wattage.

***

Abe, pushing down his fright levels the best he could, after taking several deep breaths of his own and imperceptibly lowering his heart rate, turned to face his front door, stepped forward and, just as Moxie achieved full wattage from her eyes, pulled aside two of the blinds. The impact of those golden green orbs at the very moment Abe peered out was more than the man could take.

Abe shot backwards almost with the speed of the lead balls from his double-ought shells might have achieved. He hit the bedside with the backs of his knees, spilling him ass over head completely across the mattress and onto the floor at the other side. He felt something inside crack. Abe's world, already dark enough except for Moxie's saucer-sized golden green eyes, turned black.

***

Moxie walked through the closed front door, waded through the bed and mattress without a thought, then stood tall, above Abe's inert form and waited. It was, perhaps, a few minutes, seconds maybe, but to Abe it felt as if he'd been out for years. Pretty much every nasty, mean thing he'd ever done in his cranky life passed through his dream, comma, unconscious state of mind. He was both aware, yet unaware but little mattered, because when Abe blinked once, twice, three times, then opened his eyes for real, standing above him was a creature past any imagination.

Shimmering, pearlescent hair or fur, taller than that basketball player from China, especially from Abe's perspective lying on the floor, flat on his aching back. Shining golden green eyes the size of dinner plates focused down on him, blinding him, Moxie stood. As Abe stared at her, Moxie took in a deep breath and her eyes became shop lights. Crazy stupid spots danced all around Abe's head, inside and across his eyes. Blinded by the light, so goes the song, Abe thought. Then Moxie let her breath out slowly, gently, it wafted down and into Abe's nostrils, smelling like a mix of apples and cinnamon.

Pleasant, Abe thought, momentarily distracted from the image towering above him.

Then Moxie smiled and Abe's heart stopped.

It took her awhile to absorb him, but by daylight the world had a whole new Abe to greet.

***

Abe left the apartment, not bothering to lock the door behind him. As he turned toward the gate that would take him to the sidewalk beyond, two of the lady residents walked past. They had a hurried stride and looked furtively his way.

Freshly showered and shaved, wearing slacks, shoes shining like, well, Moxie's eyes, wrinkle free shirt with a nice blue silk tie, fedora perched on his regal head, Abe cut a fine figure, dispelling the momentary nervousness of his passers by. He reached up, touching the tip of his hat and tilted his head.

"Pleasant morning to you ladies," Abe greeted them, garnishing his greeting with a brilliant smile. His teeth were incredibly white for an older man. They seemed to even glow, sort of a pearlescent quality about them. As the ladies passed by with tilts of their own heads and shy smiles, Abe passed through the gate, placed his cedar walking stick onto the sidewalk and made his way to the gate that would take him to the park out front for a restorative and invigorating walk about.

***

Unknown to Abe the ladies had paused, turned and were watching him. When he'd made the first turn of his walk and was too far to see clearly, they turned and resumed their own morning's journey. The lady with outdated blue-tinted hair turned to the one who was way too mature to have so much black hair, and smiled.

"Such a charming and distinguished looking gentleman. Such manners. So soft spoken. And did you see those incredibly white teeth? That dazzling smile?"

"Yes," her companion responded. "Just goes to show you can't always believe what the busybodies here tell you. He seemed nothing like an ogre to me."

The End?

Innocence Lost

Being eleven years old has its advantages. More advantages, thought Eddie, than disadvantages, not that others his age would agree. And certainly not based on the angst facing them all as they become teens, when they'd get into the real and serious aspects of life. But life as a teen-ager was yet ahead and for now Eddie is quite pleased with how things are going.

Lots of things are going his way. He has an allowance to die for and a somewhat successful summer business mowing lawns for MILFs in the neighborhood. Not that Eddie has any idea what that means, except that the older boys, showing off their knowledge of such things, always refer to these stay-at-home moms with their halter tops and short shorts that way.

Eddie supposes that when he turns thirteen, progressing toward fifteen, he might receive full enlightenment on the term MILF for himself. Until then, he simply enjoys that these once or future moms usually offer him milk or soda and cookies after he finishes mowing their lawns, or pausing for a break after completing the back yard.

Then, after sitting in the sunshine of his pretty-for-an-older-woman client's smile, Eddie takes to the front yard, gases up his personally-owned mower and has at it with the grass. When he's done, ready to head to the next yard — Eddie has eleven such clients. Well, one of them is a cocky older guy, twenty-five maybe, who has a couple of other guys that hang out with him a lot, — rarely ever does Eddie see any women even though the guy has a swimming pool and barbecue in his back yard. This is his twenty-fiver, but the other ten clients are very pretty women. And they all pay well, give him treats. Except for the guy, who sometimes makes Eddie nervous because he likes to play tug-o-war with the crisp twenty and five he always pays.

He lets Eddie grab it, but holds onto the bills so they don't slip away. Then, when Eddie looks up, and the guy waits for this moment, Eddie knows, the guy shoots him this funny look, then releases the bills with a quick pop, snap. Eddie gets a bit more nervous because he can feel this dude standing in the doorway, watching him push his lawn mower and gas can up the sidewalk and onward to home.

Anyway, Eddie works hard at this during his summers, starting weekends while school is going on, then working just about every day, except of course when his mom and dad take their usual summer vacation with Eddie and his older brother, Ted — who hates it and rubs the most painful goose eggs on his head when Eddie calls him Theodore — anyway, just about every day during the summer Eddie stays busy mowing lawns and making money.

Eddie has discovered that if he *hits it and gets it*, mowing three yards on Mondays and Wednesdays, two on Tuesdays and Thursdays, with the occasional exception, of course, for being sick, or sunburned, or during that vacation with the family, that leaves him with his biggest yard — the one with the guy and the swimming pool — to do on Fridays. Then voila, he has the rest of Friday and the entire weekend to dedicate to fun.

Being the enterprising person that he is though, Eddie spends certain times of the year, in the spring mostly when the dewberries and blackberries ripen, picking buckets of berries and selling them from his roadside stand. He donates some berries to his mom who creates seriously delicious blackberry and peach cobblers that they top with enough ice cream to drown a pig.

But after a tour through the local grocery store last summer with his mom, finding fresh blackberry, raspberry and blueberry containers in the fruit and vegetable section selling for nearly four bucks for maybe, ten ounces, Eddie did the math and stopped picking and selling buckets of berries for fifty-cents. No profit in it. So he just started picking enough for a few family cobblers and never again set up his roadside stand. That next spring some people who had become loyal customers even stopped by his house, knocked on the door and asked if *'the young businessman had gone out of the berry business'* to which he said yes.

But, if Eddie was having an unlucky day and his mom answered the door, she would tell them of course not and promise that her son would have a bucket of fresh-picked berries waiting for them tomorrow if they wanted to stop by and pick them up. Eddie did manage to up his price to a dollar a bucket. Eventually, though, the berry business fizzled and came to a complete stop. Fine with Eddie who recognized a labor-intensive, loss leader when he saw one.

So, during the summer, three yards for two days, two yards for two days, all at ten dollars a pop if contracted with him for the summer at twice a month, Eddie was rich. What other kid in his school made a hundred bucks a week mowing ten yards, then picked up a twenty-fiver on Friday, saved one-hundred dollars of it for his *college fund* — what's the deal with parents forcing their kids to pay their own tuition, aren't they supposed to do that? — and kept the other for his own spending money? Dad was always using terms like *fiscal responsibility* and *mature behavior* but Eddie often worried that his parents might run low on funds and raid his stash.

That hadn't happened yet, and just for taking out the trash, sweeping out the garage once a month, drying dishes while dad did his once-a-week volunteer turn at washing dishes, Eddie took in another ten dollars a week. And this income is year round folks. So, he figured if things got really tight and his dad needed some help, all he had to do was ask and Eddie would help.

It was Ted that really had Eddie worried. He had no doubt whatsoever that if Ted ever learned where his younger brother hid his money jar the cash would vanish like vapor. A time or two, when dad worked with Eddie to fill out his deposit slip and check figures in his savings account book, Eddie felt like there wasn't quite as much money totaled for the deposit as there should have been, especially during summers when the cash flow was awesome. He suspected, but had not yet caught, Ted dipping into those hard-earned funds so Eddie never got around to making any accusations. Still, he found it necessary to locate inventive new hideaways for his money jar.

For a time Eddie took to burying the jar out back but he worried that somebody's dog, a nosey kid, or Ted might be messing around with a shovel or something — well the dog would use his paws, of course but the others would dink around with a shovel, right? — and discover his money. That wouldn't be so bad early in the month, just after making one of his savings account deposits at the bank with dad, but just before deposit time, when the jar was stuffed. The loss would be catastrophic.

Then one day everything turned to crap. Crap was the word Eddie used because mom usually gave him a pass on that one so long as he didn't use it extensively or several times in a row on any given day. The "S" word and most assuredly not the "F" word — something his older brother had become fondly attached to lately, especially when rubbing a painful egg on Eddie's head — were off limits for anyone under the age of *accountability*. Accountability? Eddie often wondered if that word had something to do with the likes of *fiscal responsibility* or *mature behavior*. When he asked his dad one time what it meant, dad said it was 'a Biblical expression'

Whatever that means. Confusing, really, since dad used it a lot whenever he was helping Eddie do his savings deposit slip, figuring totals or sometimes at his desk, balancing his own, or mom's checkbook.

Another interesting word for Eddie was *reconciled* and he noted that dad used the term most often when trying to help mom out by balancing her checkbook and account. The term was usually in a sentence that went 'how is it, Honey, that I can never seem to *reconcile* your balance?' Mom was of the notion that it didn't matter about balancing her checkbook or reconciling the balance. She often told dad that she went by what the deposit receipts showed whenever she put some more in or took some more out.

"I don't understand why we need to concern ourselves with that headache when the totals are right there on my deposit and withdrawal slips," she often exclaimed when dad posed questions about purchases and totals in a slightly different tone of voice. It was the same tone of voice he sometimes took with Eddie or Ted when he was close to the boiling point. That rarely occurred but when it did it was usually because the boys pretended to not understand whatever point it was dad was attempting to get across. Or, of course, the few times they actually got caught doing something off-limits, or when Ted would walk away muttering what sounded an awful lot like the "F" word.

Anyway, on this one particular day in the middle of summer, shortly after they'd returned from the annual vacation, everything turned to crap. The first revelation of this was when Eddie pulled his money jar down from the very top of the closet in mom's wash room, out from behind the blankets and quilts she stored there for the summer. It was always light in heft because it nearly always held bills and rarely much change. The predominance of denomination was ten dollar bills, with some ones, fives and the occasional twenty. There were nearly always a couple of twenty dollar bills in the jar. But this time not only were there no twenty's but the ten dollar bills seemed a bit low as well.

This didn't ring well for Eddie. He decided, however, to put his jar back where it had been hidden, only he rigged up a little trap. There were some old mouse and rat traps in the garage. Eddie took several of the smaller ones and a couple of the bigger ones and went about setting them. He placed them carefully all about the top shelf so that any unsuspecting older brother would likely get his fingers snapped by at least one while reaching up to grab the money jar.

Only problem was Theodore had already conducted his raid for the time being and it was dad who decided to rummage around on the upper shelves, looking for some old cap or something. From all the howling and cursing that went on after a couple of loud trap snaps, and something else getting knocked off one of the other shelves — dad's old fishing tackle box, thought Eddie — the silence was scary. Dad came into the house with a fierce scowl on his face, Eddie's money jar tucked under one arm, sprung traps dangling from the other hand.

Eddie tried to explain but dad would have none of it. He confiscated the money jar, with the money inside it, and informed Eddie that if he couldn't trust family — and he damned well knew who Eddie had set the traps for, his brother — then he couldn't trust anybody. The announcement was made that from this day forward Eddie would turn over his savings money at the end of any day he received money and his dad would handle the funds.

Eddie figured that wasn't any better than trying to hide the money jar from his brother. Only instead of outright stealing his dough, dad would simply shove it into his pocket without keeping count, expecting Eddie to be keeping track in a ledger, whereupon the money would get mixed with his dad's funds. Try to convince dad that had happened, thought Eddie. But the one attempt he made to convince his dad there had to be a better, safer, more secure way to handle his hard-earned wages brought a really, serious version of dad's *look* so Eddie clammed up. He figured he'd wait things out until some semblance of normal returned, then go back to the way things had been before.

The crappy day, however, was just starting. Eddie's dad had only found a couple of the traps, the rest remained where Eddie had placed them, locked and loaded. And shortly after the confrontation with his dad, Theodore, moving up the schedule for another visit to Eddie's money jar did, in fact, come into contact with the remaining traps. When dad pulled them apart, before Ted was about to kill his younger brother, it was Eddie who got punished. He was sent to his room.

How fair is that?

Problem is it was also the room he shared with Theodore and Theodore kept finding reasons to come into the room, putting a goose egg on Eddie's head and arms with knuckle bumps that really, actually hurt. Eddie kept his yelps silent and his tears to himself. He knew any further show of aggression would only make matters worse during the night. It wouldn't be the first time his older brother snuck over to Eddie's twin bed and sucker punched him in the arm while he was dead asleep.

Then mom calls up to him, laying there in the dark room, between visits from Ted, and says "that lovely Mrs. Patterson called and wants to know if you'll come by now and trim her sidewalks and flower beds for her. She's having guests over and she doesn't want them to arrive while there's still sunlight and seeing the overgrown grass and weeds. She'll pay you extra," Mom called out.

So, Eddie took advantage of his reprieve from dad's punishment and Ted's continued torture, went down to the garage and grabbed the new hedger and edger tool he'd recently purchased. Not knowing for sure if he'd need the mower, Eddie brought that as well. When he got to the Patterson's residence Eddie couldn't see where any trimming was needed. So, he knocks on the door and when one of Ted's MILF references answers, wearing what looks like a bath towel wrapped around her, barely covering top or bottom, only the unimportant stuff between, Eddie stammers and stutters about not seeing any need for additional trimming.

"Silly boy," Mrs. Patterson says, reaching out and patting him on the head, very nearly releasing the towel wrapped around her. "Oops," she smiles at him, hands him a ten dollar bill from the table by the door, tells him to do a good job, then turns and walks away. Eddie, not one to argue against a ten dollar bonus, turns to the task at hand. When he finished trimming grass that wasn't there, mowing a bit from under the hedge that bordered the Patterson and Hemling residences, just in case it was a quarter-inch taller than it should be, Eddie went back to the partially opened front door to knock, then ask to borrow a broom to sweep the sidewalk and driveway.

Only, when Eddie rang the doorbell, then knocked, he got no answer. He knew from previous experiences though, where the broom closet was. After all, he'd had milk, cola, cookies and sometimes a pimento cheese sandwich at the kitchen table before. Eddie pushed the door that Mrs. Patterson had left partially open and tip-toed toward the broom closet.

That was when he glanced through the hallway, into a side room and saw Mrs. Patterson *without* the towel, standing in front of a mirror and checking herself out. More from curiosity than lechery, if he even knew what that meant, Eddie froze in his tracks and stared, mouth agape. At the same time Mrs. Patterson looked up to see him standing there staring, Mr. Patterson walked through the front door.

"Hey you little peepsqueak," Mr. Patterson barked. Eddie yelped and the lovely Mrs. Patterson smoothly stepped away from the mirror and door, out of sight. Stammering that he'd only intended to get a shop broom so he could sweep the grass off the driveway and sidewalk, Eddie backed into a wall and bumped his head, which forced his mouth to shut hard, biting his tongue, which made him yelp again.

"Don't blame you for staring, Eddie," Mr. Patterson said. "Go get your broom and take care of business."

So, humiliated, embarrassed and still seriously curious about Mrs. Patterson, Eddie hustled to the broom closet without further mishap, retrieved the necessary item and quickly made his exit. He heard a tinkle of laughter from the lady of the house, followed by a lecherous — Eddie now knew, probably he thought, what that word meant — burst of laughter from the mister as he closed the front door behind him.

Then the broom handle broke. Right in half, making the job twice as hard. But Eddie for sure was determined to not get caught in the house again, at least not twice on the same day. He had his money, but something nibbled at the back of his mind, increasing his curiosity about the nudity he'd recently witnessed, developing a subconscious determination to repeat the experience first chance he got.

Then, just when it seemed all would end well enough, one of his other clients saw Eddie roll past with his lawn care tools. The day had gone bad enough, starting with the mouse trap fiasco that was supposed to catch Ted, not his dad, and having to work extra on a Friday when he hadn't planned it. Now, exhausted from the series of weird things happening to him, mentally and physically, Eddie hears Mrs. Hollister calling out in her husky voice.

"Eddie! Oh, Eddie! Can you help me out here?"

Reluctantly, Eddie turns up the driveway to the Hollister door where Mrs. Holister, every bit as pretty as Mrs. Patterson, but bigger in places and less subtle about showing it off. Her mane of fiery red hair and the bounty of freckles on all the exposed skin Eddie could see were something to behold.

"Yes ma'am," Eddie responded. "What ya need?"

Well, another ten dollars to the good, Eddie only had to trim the lady's hedge on one side and the top. "Oh they can do their own side, or pay you to do it, I suppose," Mrs. Hollister said of the neighbors. "Let it go."

The whole time Eddie was doing her trimming, Mrs. Hollister sat on her front porch, painting her toenails a bright, flaming red that matched her hair. She'd look up to see him casting furtive glances her way, raising up and throwing him a knowing smile when she noticed where he'd been looking so furtively.

Eddie didn't really understand what this was all about except that he knew a dose of two pretty older women in one day was just a bit more than any healthy eleven-year-old should have to deal with. Especially not knowing what, exactly, it was he was dealing with.

The day wasn't over though.

"Put it in there," dad said, as Eddie walked in the house after he finished putting away his lawn care tools and knocked off the loose grass from his tennis shoes. Dad pointed at Eddie's money jar sitting there on his desk for all the world, and Theodore, to see.

"What?"

"You picked up some extra money today, working

for the Pattersons, and Barbara Hollister called while you were out, said she'd catch you when you passed by when we told her you were doing some yard work up the street, at the Patterson house." Dad pointed again in the general direction of his home office and desk. "So, buddy, drop it in your jar. We'll tally it up this weekend. You can ride with me Monday to the bank and we'll make another deposit to your account. How much you got now, anyway?"

Eddied mumbled something about not being sure and managed to slip one of the ten dollar bills into his jar while keeping the other one wadded up in the bottom of his pocket. No way was he going to put all his money in that jar just so his butt head brother could rip him off later. Eddie turned the corner and dashed up the stairs before his dad could think to check his pockets or stop him for some other perceived infraction.

That was when he walked in unexpectedly, apparently, on his older brother, catching him shoving something under his mattress. Eddie pretended not to notice, pulled open his t-shirt drawer and pulled out a clean one. The jeans would do for the rest of the evening since he had no plans for going anywhere, seeing anybody. It was family television night unless he and or Ted could figure a way out of it. Likely, though, if they didn't settle for watching some stupid show or, worse yet, the evening news — dad always insisted his boys *stay on top of things* about this country and the world — they'd get stuck playing Yatzee, Monopoly or, gasp, one-on-one checkers with dad while mom got a bye.

Sometimes dad made mom and Ted sit with them and watch while he pretended to have a hard time at beating Eddie with all his double-decker kings against the one or three surviving checkers his son had on the board. Most of the time it went fast and Eddie went down in flames, but there were times, like probably tonight, with dad in a particularly aggressive mood, dad might drag the game out for what feel like hours. Theodore, Eddie thought, always made it worse by guffawing when he lost. Mom added insult to injury by suggesting openly, to Ted's delight, that Eddie would probably win next time. "You're getting so good, honey."

Eddie got his game on when he slipped three of the mouse traps into the foot of his brother's bed, under the cover sheet, and a couple of the larger rat traps under the mattress, where Eddie discovered three of the missing twenty's from his money jar, crumpled up in little balls. Little brother exchanged the traps for the twenty dollar bills. He replaced the crumpled twenty's with three crumpled one dollar bills — let Theodore figure that one out, Eddie smiled at the thought.

***

Word must have gotten out because for the next two weeks of lawn mowing, trimming and clearing, his lady clients were all smiles, occasional giggles and more exposed than ever before. Eddie quickly figured that Mrs. Patterson or Mrs. Hollister, or both, had been engaging in some talk about their yard man and his proclivity for scoping out the older women in the neighborhood. He absolutely *knew* that was the case when the most absolutely gorgeous by far, the youngest looking of them and the one with the softest, warmest voice and greenest eyes was particularly attentive, constantly bending over and picking up stuff — imaginary, Eddie thought — off the floor. Some bit or particle of whatever that, presumably, Eddie had tracked in from the yard. She even stood across from him on the other side of her little breakfast table and leaned over onto it, elbows planted and hands under her chin. Nothing was left to his imagination, based on what Eddie knew of the female anatomy. It didn't appear as if she had the slightest idea of what was being exposed there.

On the other hand, Mrs. Olivetti kept looking him directly in the eyes making Eddie so darned nervous he finally made good his escape by spilling the last of his milk, apologizing hastily and dashing out the door, yelping that he had one more stop to make before his work was done. Eddie thought he heard Mrs. Olivetti chuckle softly.

***

The night after he retrieved his money from Ted's mattress and left the traps behind, his brother reached in there when he thought little bro was sound asleep. If Eddie had been asleep, he was wide awake when Ted let out a yelp, then pounced on top of him and started knuckle-punching him all over the arms and legs, rubbing his knuckles hard across Eddie's head.

Dad burst in and demanded that they quiet down or he was going to make them both 'rue the day you were born' slammed the door shut, causing the night light to pop right out of its socket and one of Ted's plastic model airplanes tacked to the ceiling take a death-dealing dive to their night stand, then onto the floor in a supreme display of total destruction.

Eddie quickly stepped over the field of debris as he

watched his brother slip into his bed, wary of doing anything more that might bring down the Wrath of Dad. He heard the mouse traps go off as Theodore slipped his toes deep into the recesses of his cover sheet, made it to their bathroom and locked the door before his brother could catch him. It was close, but Eddie knew his brother was not going to make more noise for dad to hear, or mom to complain about.

Eddie spent the next two hours sitting in the locked bathroom, reading from his comic book stash kept in the bottom of the dirty clothes hamper. If Ted ever discovered them he'd trash them, so Eddie knew that, like his money jar, if he wanted them to remain safe from his brother, they had to be kept someplace his brother was not likely to venture. Theodore never placed his discarded clothing inside the hamper — something mom harped on him about daily.

Eddie lost track of time, sitting there, waiting for things to settle down and his brother to go to sleep. He had no idea how long it would take for Ted to simmer down enough for his eyes to get heavy. Without realizing it, Eddie's eyes, also, were getting heavy. He fell off the toilet lid.

Rubbing the resulting goose egg, worse than any Ted

had ever dealt him, Eddie cautiously made his way to his bed while tears continued to flow. Ted was out for the night, he hoped, and so he slipped into his own sheets after first searching to see if any traps had been set and placed there in retaliation. Eddie slipped back out of bed, having spied the traps stacked on the night stand, grabbed them and hid them under his spare pillow, then slipped back under the covers and almost immediately feel into a deep, dream-filled sleep.

***

The dreams were more like nightmares, and most of them had older women scratching at him, running after him, grabbing at him as he ran down a long, narrow sidewalk. There was a line of them, several looking a lot like his lawn business clients, lined up on both sides of the sidewalk. He couldn't run very fast and every time it looked as if he'd make it past this gauntlet of women with their painted, spooky faces, one would trip him up with a rake or broom handle and another would grab and rip his t-shirt. His favorite t-shirt for gosh sakes.

Then Mrs. Hollister, Olevetti and Patterson were all holding him down, tickling him. Everywhere! Eddie woke himself up, yelling.

He quickly glanced over at his brother's bed but no movement there. He listened quietly, not daring to breathe, for footsteps from his mom and dad's bedroom. Nothing. Great, he thought, a burglar could climb in the window and try to kidnap me and nobody here would even notice, even if I bit him on the hand covering my mouth and screamed like a girl.

The resulting bad mood at having been totally ignored while getting kidnapped from his own bed kept further nightmares at bay. An exhausted Eddie woke up Saturday morning before his brother, got dressed and made good his escape. He left a note for his mom, saying he was going to go exploring the nearby bayou with some friends, maybe hunt for frogs, and left it stuck to the fridge with one of her magnets. A covered glass filled with milk and four Pop-Tarts generated breakfast and all the immediate supply of energy he desired. Eddie was gone to embrace the day.

***

All went well for Eddie over the next few weeks. Well, except for the ongoing stuff being pulled by his lawn care clients. They made Eddie's life miserable on two levels, frustrating him because he *wanted* to look when they weren't paying attention, and frustrating him by *looking* at him when he didn't want them to catch him staring. It also bothered Eddie that it mattered to him at all. What did he care if this or that flopped out, was totally visible or flesh was flashed, intentionally or by accident? What Eddie hated most is that it seemed as if they were doing this on purpose. Eddie supposed he could weather it out, summer was drawing to a close and school would start up soon. But still, they were having fun with him and Eddie did not appreciate that.

That kind of stuff was so totally not right, Eddie thought. Not that his parents were prudes or anything, whatever *prude* means, but neither of them went around flashing it at him, or Ted. More so Ted because he was already more lecherous than a kid his age had a right to be, older brother or not. Sure, Eddie had picked up a peek-a-boo a time or two over the years, but it passed so quickly he never really ever realized what he was seeing.

Dad thought he did a fairly good job hiding the girly magazines he liked to collect, both from mom and from the boys, but Ted found his stash early on. Ted, when in a decent frame of mind, or not, would then take advantage of his superior knowledge of the female anatomy and dad's magazines to educate Eddie who, mostly was so not interested. Some of what Ted said was actually pretty gross, you think about it deeply enough. Yuck!

Years down the road Eddie would come to learn that at age eleven he was just about the right age to learn some of this stuff, however inaccurate the information or reliable the source. But for now he was quite sure he wasn't supposed to know the non-medical terms for all that stuff. Ted probably used those terms instead of medical terms because he had enough trouble reading, much less pronouncing anatomically correct descriptive medical terms for anybody's body parts.

***

The next summer, when his clients took to telling Eddie how 'cute' he looked when he turned all red while rubbing suntan lotion on their backs for them — how could they know with their backs to his face? Or how his freckles 'popped out' when he accidentally — on their intentional miscue — caught a major glimpse of this, that or the other. But when they started kissing him on the cheek while tucking his money in his pockets, Eddie decided older women simply were not in his game plan. At least not in the far distant future. So, at the end of the summer run he advised all his clients he was moving forward with his business enterprises and they should start looking for another young entrepreneur — that wasn't the word Eddie used but he had heard it and knew what it meant — and he would help them find a good replacement.

They all made goofy faces, silly noises and pouted with great exaggeration but Eddie stood his ground, telling them he'd accepted a neighborhood newspaper route, and if they wanted to subscribe to the paper he was working for, they'd still get to enjoy working with him. Eddie figured this was safe enough because he could simply pedal right past each address without stopping, or wave as he rolled by. He'd only have to confront them once a month to collect.

***

It was not his Summer of '42, that would come in a few more years, maybe, but Eddie would look back longingly on that eleventh year summer, when he made his own money, stood up to his brother and learned all about women. Well, enough anyway.

www.ingramcontent.com/pod-product-compliance
Ingram Content Group UK Ltd.
Pitfield, Milton Keynes, MK11 3LW, UK
UKHW020220250726
13967UKWH00001B/108

9 781300 351603